# THE HOCKEY MACHINE

THE #1
SPORTS SERIES
FOR KIDS

# THE HOCKEY MACHINE

**LITTLE, BROWN AND COMPANY**
New York Boston

Little, Brown and Company

Hachette Book Group
1290 Avenue of the Americas, New York, NY 10104
Visit our website at www.lb-kids.com

www.mattchristopher.com

Little, Brown and Company is a division of Hachette Book Group, Inc.
The Little, Brown name and logo are trademarks of Hachette Book Group, Inc.

The publisher is not responsible for websites (or their content) that are not owned by the publisher.

First Paperback Edition: September 1992
First published in hardcover in October 1986 by Little, Brown and Company

The characters and events in this book are fictitious. Any similarity to real persons, living or dead, is coincidental and not intended by the author.

Matt Christopher® is a registered trademark of
Matt Christopher Royalties, Inc.

Library of Congress Cataloging-in-Publication Data

Christopher, Matt.
        The hockey machine.
        Summary: Abducted by a "fan" and forced to become a member of a
professional junior hockey team, thirteen-year-old star center Steve Crandell
quickly realizes that he must play not only to win but to survive.

        ISBN 978-0-316-14087-4
        [1. Hockey — Fiction.    2. Mystery and detective stories.]
        I. Title.
        PZ7.C458Ho   1986   [Fic]                                87-3714

30 29 28 27 26 25

RRD-C

Printed in the United States of America

To Duane and Karen

# THE HOCKEY MACHINE

# 1

The sharp, glistening ice skates almost slid out from under Steve Crandall as he banged into the boards flanking the curved sides of the rink. Keeping his balance, he caromed off the boards and sped after the loose puck.

He and the flashy Buckeye center, Jack Finlay, reached it at the same time. Realizing that Jack had a better chance of getting the puck than he, Steve rammed into him with a body check. A grunt tore from Jack as the blow sent him sprawling onto the ice.

Steve hooked the puck with his stick and carried it across the blue line into neutral territory. As two Buckeyes charged at him he passed the puck to right wingman Eddie Traynor.

Just then one of the Buckeyes' skates struck Steve's left skate, knocking him off balance. He fell and skidded on the ice in a slow spin. Disgusted, he scrambled to his feet, glanced around, and saw Eddie pass the puck to Stu Pierce, the Buckeyes' tall, speedy left wingman.

The pass was a poor one. The puck zipped behind Stu where he couldn't get it in spite of his quick, ice-flying stop. It ricocheted against the boards back into the face-off circle. A Buckeyes' defenseman intercepted it and slapped it toward the boards in an effort to put it back into Bobtails' territory.

But Steve could see a play in the making. He skated almost to the exact spot where he expected the puck to ricochet on the ice, hooked it with his stick and dribbled it down alongside the rink. He hardly kept his eyes on it as he stickhandled it, moving the hard rubber disk forward with expert, back-and-forth movements.

He saw the Buckeyes' goalie crouched in the crease near the corner of the goal. A Buckeyes' defenseman stood at the goalie's left side, also waiting for an anticipated shot. So far, with the game in the middle of the third period, Steve had racked up five points out of the seven that the Bobtails had scored. What's wrong with shooting for a sixth? he thought.

The open space to the left of the goalie was Steve's target. It wasn't a big one, but he had scored in smaller ones.

Just as a Buckeyes' wingman charged at him, Steve slapped the puck with a hard, solid blow. The disk rose off the ice and flew toward the open space so fast only a few pairs of eyes were able to follow it. Both the defensive man and the goalie raised their gloved hands in a desperate try to catch it, then dropped them helplessly as the puck sailed into the corner of the net for Steve's sixth point.

The Bobtails' fans roared, joining the thunder that rose from the boards against which Lines Two and Three were banging their sticks.

"Hey, man! Two hat tricks in one game! You're cooking!" sweaty-faced Eddie Traynor cried, smiling broadly as he skated up alongside of Steve.

Steve smiled back, his hazel eyes twinkling, his heart pounding under the blue shirt of his uniform. He wiped off the sweat that rolled down his own tired face and wished he didn't have to wear that hot helmet. But rules were rules.

3

"Just lucky," he said.

"Lucky, my eye," Eddie replied. "You're good, man."

"Thanks, Eddie," said Steve modestly.

Steve had learned to skate when he was four years old. He had had a good teacher — his father. Edgar Crandall had played hockey in college and taught his young son to skate with hopes that someday he, too, would play college hockey.

But Steve's ability had turned out to be even better than Edgar Crandall had expected. "I think you would've turned out to be an excellent skater even if I hadn't taught you," he had told Steve one day. "Keep it up and someday you'll wind up as another Wayne Gretzky or Mike Bossy."

Steve knew of Gretzky and Bossy. They were two of the greatest hockey scorers ever. "That'll be the day, Dad," he said grinning.

Steve had worked hard at being the best he could, hustling every minute, making every opportunity count, and — just as important — keeping himself in excellent physical condition by practicing constantly, eating well, and getting plenty of sleep. But the real key was his love of the game.

Line One of both teams played another minute, then relinquished the ice to the second lines. Steve, holding his helmet and stick, watched from behind the boards as both lines tried to score but didn't.

The Bobtails' Line Three did no better. They gave up one score fifty seconds before they got off the ice. Bobtails 8, Buckeyes 3.

Line One returned to the ice one last time. Feeling fresh and raring to go again, Steve, at center, gave the puck a hard poke as the referee dropped it at the blow of the whistle.

Jack Finlay, the Buckeyes' tall, bony center, struck the puck at the same time. Both hockey sticks clashed and clattered as they missed or connected with the puck. At last the disk shot across the Buckeyes' blue line where a Buckeye wingman hooked it with his stick and sent it skittering toward a teammate at the other side of the rink. Rudy Pollack, the Bobtails' defenseman, sped after it and passed it to Jim Hogan, the other Bobtails' defenseman.

But just then a husky Buckeye crashed into him with a neat body check, hooked his stick around the puck, and carried it toward the Bobtails' goal.

He was fast and handled the puck expertly. Steve,

speeding across the blue line after him, had a hunch that the player intended to go for a score by himself.

Adding on an extra burst of speed, Steve caught up to him just as the player was about to take a hard swing at the puck.

"Look out!" Steve yelled as he sped past the player.

The Buckeye, his concentration disrupted, paused for just an instant as he glanced at Steve. Then he lashed out at the puck. Too late. Steve grabbed it with his stick as he flew by, skated in a half-circle, then stickhandled the disk back up the ice. Two men raced after him. He passed to Eddie as a roar exploded from the Bobtails' fans, praising Steve for getting the puck back into Bobtails' possession.

Sweat beaded on Steve's lips and forehead. He took his time skating up the ice, remembering his father's wise advice to "reserve your energy at the right times." Yet, when he was taking his time, he was almost as fast as some of the other players who were skating their fastest.

He took off with a burst of speed as left wingman Stu Pierce, receiving a pass from Eddie, bolted toward the net. Both of the Buckeyes' defensemen and their goalie put up a defensive wall against him.

"Stu!" Steve yelled as he skated up alongside of him.

Stu passed to him. Steve caught the puck, skated around the back of the net, and quickly passed it back to Stu. In a surprise move Stu stopped it with his stick, then flipped it toward the corner of the net, missing the goalie's right shoulder by inches.

Another score! This time Stu got the point and Steve the assist.

A call from Coach Larry Hall, standing behind the boards, was the signal for Line One to get off the ice and Line Two to replace them.

Four minutes later the game was over, with the Bobtails winning it 9 to 3.

Handshakes and shoulder pats greeted the Bobtails on their way to the locker room. After Steve showered and changed into his regular clothes he left the building, anxious to get home to fill his hunger-gnawing stomach. The late Saturday afternoon sun was slowly disappearing over the western horizon. The shadows were long, the November air crisp. The only signs of last week's snow were the white spots that clung to some roofs and corners the sun couldn't reach.

Steve, his blond hair still damp behind his neck, started to climb down the steps of Manley Rink when a boy about his age stepped up beside him. He was tall, well dressed, and wore leather gloves.

"Hi, Steve," he said, his brown eyes smiling. "I'm Mark Slate. You played a terrific game."

Steve frowned, bewildered. "Thanks," he said. Mark Slate? I don't know of any Mark Slate, he thought.

"I know you don't know me," Mark said, reading Steve's mind, "but I've watched you play in several games already, and . . . well . . . I feel almost as if I've know you for a long time."

"You've been watching *me* play? Why?" Steve looked again at the sharp clothes this Mark Slate wore, the expensive leather gloves. Something in the back of his mind began to creep into focus. He remembered now seeing Mark at some of the games, sitting in a seat on the top row, dressed very much as he was dressed now.

Mark's smile broadened. "For a good reason," he

said. "And perfectly legitimate, believe me. Come on. I want to introduce you to a friend of mine, Kenneth Agard, Jr. He's over there, sitting in that car."

Steve looked at a shiny, black automobile parked at the curb, at the man sitting behind the wheel wearing a chauffeur's cap.

"You can't see Kenneth from here," said Mark. "He's sitting in the back seat."

He headed down the steps. Steve started to follow him, then paused. "I can't," he said.

Mark looked at him. "Why not? There's nothing to be afraid of. Kenneth is a good kid, and a genius when it comes to hockey. He just wants to talk —"

"I've got to get home," Steve cut in. "My parents are expecting me." He didn't want to say that they had warned him dozens of times not to trust strangers. Mark must have heard that same warning dozens of times himself.

"Look, I know what you're thinking," Mark said. His voice was calm, friendly. "Don't trust strangers. Well, I don't blame you. But Kenneth Agard, Jr., is no stranger. He knows who you are, even though you don't know who he is. And he's as honest as the day is long. Take my word for it." He took Steve by

9

the arm. "Come on. I guarantee you'll like him and what he has to tell you. I promise."

Steve studied Mark's face, saw the genuine look of friendliness in it, and felt as if he had known Mark a long time, too. Maybe I'm being too cautious, he thought. Mark seems like a real nice trustworthy guy.

"Okay," Steve said. "I'll see your friend. But I can't stay long."

"Good," Mark said. "Come on."

# 2

They got to the car, and Mark politely opened the rear door. "Kenneth, meet Steve Crandall," he said. "Steve, this is my friend, Kenneth Agard, Jr."

Steve barely heard him. He was looking at the shine on the limousine, at his reflection in it, then at the luxurious, bright-red interior. Boy, this Kenneth Agard guy must be *rich*, he thought.

His head was still swimming as he glanced at the boy in the back seat. Kenneth was dressed as neatly as Mark, but his smile, his well-groomed black hair, and his brilliant brown eyes behind stylish glasses, indicated to Steve that there was something special about him. Certainly nothing to distrust.

"Hi, Steve," Kenneth said, extending a hand. "I'm pleased to meet you. Come on, get in."

Steve remained standing, giving Kenneth a closer look. I can't believe it, he thought. He's not more than a year or so older than I am. Yet, he seems a lot older.

"Here, let me take your bag," said Mark.

Steve found himself handing the bag to Mark. Then he watched, wonderingly, as Mark carried it to the trunk of the car.

"Get in," Kenneth Agard, Jr., repeated. "We'll give you a lift home, and talk on the way. Okay?"

Steve put a foot inside the car. "Talk about what?"

"Hockey," Kenneth answered. "That's your favorite sport, isn't it?"

Steve was hardly aware that Kenneth was gently helping him into the car. He sat down beside Kenneth as he heard the trunk door slam shut. Then Mark came to the side of the car, closed the back seat door, and climbed in front with the driver. Instantly the car started up and eased away from the curb.

"I have an idea," Kenneth said. "We'll stop at a restaurant first. We'll eat, *then* we'll take you home. I'm sure you're hungry enough to eat a horse, right?" His eyes danced as he looked at Steve.

"No, I shouldn't," Steve said. "I have to get back home. My parents —"

"Don't worry about it," Kenneth broke in evenly. "Everything will be all right. Take my word for it. How does steak sound to you?"

Steve shrugged. He hadn't had steak and onions in ages. "Good," he said. "But, really, I —"

Kenneth gave him a friendly pat. "Fine. The Tel-Man Restaurant, Mike," Kenneth said to the driver.

Steve's mouth was still open as he looked at Kenneth, then, as if in a daze, he gazed out the car window. This Agard guy certainly didn't let any grass grow under his feet, he thought. They drove outside of Water Falls and parked in front of the elegant Tel-Man Restaurant. Steve was familiar with it. He'd been there a few times with his parents, but *never* for steak.

They all got out of the car. Kenneth introduced the driver to Steve as simply "Mike, my chauffeur," then all four of them entered the restaurant. A waitress led them to a table, handed them a menu, and said she'd be back in a minute.

"Order whatever you like," Kenneth said to Steve. "It's on me."

Steve stared at him. "I don't get it," he said curi-
ous. "Why are you doing this?"

Kenneth smiled. "To get better acquainted. Why
else?"

Why? thought Steve. Why should we get better
acquainted?

The waitress returned. The boys and the chauffeur gave her their orders, then Kenneth talked
about the Bobtails-Buckeyes hockey game. He was
really impressed by Steve's performance, he said.

"You're even better than what the sports writers
say about you," he said, his eyes flashing behind his
glasses. "I'm more than an aficionado, Steve. My father was a college star, just like your father was. He
taught me a lot about hockey, but mainly about the
business end of it, which I'm mostly interested in."

Steve looked at him, feeling uncertain. Kenneth
interested in the business end of hockey? Incredi-
ble. Wasn't that an adult's job? And then Steve remembered that Mark had said something about
Kenneth being some kind of genius. Maybe it made
sense. He wasn't sure.

Their dinners came. They ate, talking very little

now. He seems to know a lot about me, Steve thought. And about my family.

When they finished, Kenneth paid the check with cash and left a sizable tip. "How do you feel now?" he asked Steve.

"Full," replied Steve. Is this it? he wondered. Did he take me to dinner just to tell me how impressed he was about my playing?

They left the restaurant and got back into the car. Steve couldn't remember ever having eaten so much steak and onions. He felt so full and contented he was sure he could fall asleep in five seconds if he closed his eyes.

It wasn't until a couple of minutes later that he realized the car wasn't heading for Water Falls, but in the opposite direction. A cold chill rippled through him. What was Kenneth up to? He had promised to give me a lift home, Steve thought, glancing aside at the boy genius sitting next to him.

"Where are we going now?" he wanted to know. All at once he was nervous, frightened. Kenneth hadn't said that they'd be going anywhere else.

"We're going to the airport, Steve," said Kenneth,

as calmly as if he were talking about the weather. "And then flying to Indiana. Now, just take it easy. There's nothing to worry about, I promise you. If it'll make you feel any better, your parents know about this and are totally agreeable to your coming with me."

Steve stared at him. Kenneth seemed so *decent*, Steve thought, but was that decency just make-believe? How could he know?

"Why can't I see them first?" he asked, the chill gripping his spine getting even colder.

"Because we don't have time," Kenneth said. He took a letter out of his pocket and handed it to Steve. "Here, read it," he said. "It's from your father to me."

Steve took the letter, unfolded it, and saw that it had been typed. It could've been written by anybody, he thought. But the signature below it was definitely his father's.

*Dear Mr. Agard, Jr.,* (he read)

*Thanks for your very kind words about our son Steve. We feel that he has potential as a future hockey star, too, and my wife and I are in complete agreement in permitting him to go with you to Indiana for further development. Providing a private school for his education solves that problem, indeed. However, although we have signed the agreement, whether or not he goes is his decision.*

*Your pay offer is generous, and we will see to it that it goes into a special trust fund for Steve, providing he accepts your offer, of course.*

> *Best wishes,*
> *Edgar Crandall*

Steve stared at Kenneth. Letter or not, something seemed fishy about this whole thing, he thought. That signature *looked* like his father's, but it could have been forged. Another thing: why hadn't his parents said anything to him about this? They must have known before today's game about the deal Kenneth Agard, Jr., had planned for him.

"No! I won't go with you!" he shouted, shaking the letter at Kenneth. "How do I know you're not kidnappers? What're you going to do? Send a ransom note —"

"No, no, no," Kenneth said, grabbing the letter away from Steve. "You're letting your imagination run away with you. Just a minute. Let me show you something."

While Kenneth reached into the briefcase beside him, Mark Slate said, "Steve, I told you not to worry. Please trust us. We're not kidnapping you, or anything crazy like that. Kenneth has just recognized a potential hockey star in you and wants to do all he can in developing it, that's all."

"Sure," said Steve. "If I believe that, I'd believe anything."

"Then *believe*," Kenneth Agard, Jr., said, as he handed Steve a book he'd taken from his briefcase. It was a scrapbook, filled with articles about Steve's team — more than he knew ever existed — and photographs of Steve taking swiping shots at a puck, each one different, showing his aggressiveness, ability, and love for the game.

Steve looked at them, stunned. "Who took these pictures?" he asked.

"I did," Mark said, and grinned. "Now do you believe?"

"I — I'm not sure," Steve said.

He handed the scrapbook back to Kenneth, leaned back, and gazed out of the window. Those articles and pictures of him were genuine, all right. Strong evidence that Kenneth Agard, Jr., was sincere in his appreciation of Steve's hockey playing ability. But did that mean he could take Steve away like this? Take him to Indiana?

They finally arrived at the airport. It was so small it boasted only two runways. Mike, the chauffeur, entered the small terminal building and emerged a few minutes later with a piece of paper he put into his jacket pocket. Then all four of them walked to a sleek, white, twin-engined jet airplane parked alongside two smaller airplanes and got in.

Mike sat at the controls, Mark beside him. Steve and Kenneth sat behind them. They fastened their seatbelts and Mike started up the engines. After a few sputtering coughs the engines began to run smoothly. The plane taxied down the runway and in a minute it was airborne.

"Where exactly are we going to in Indiana?" Steve asked, glancing at Kenneth.

"The name of the town makes no difference. The place does," Kenneth answered. "It's the biggest, most beautiful ice rink you'll ever see."

# 3

**L**ess than hour later Steve felt a slight bump and the *zip-zip* sound of the tires as the plane landed on a private airport in country surroundings. He was still baffled by what was happening to him, as if this were all a dream. A bad nightmare. Maybe he'd wake up and find that it *was* a dream. But he knew better. It was real. It was all too real.

Mike taxied the plane into a hangar that housed a smaller plane, and everyone got out and into a car that was parked outside. Mike started it, and drove across the runway to a macadam road, speeding ahead with headlights piercing the fast falling darkness.

In less than five minutes they slowed down, drove into a long, tree-flanked private driveway, and parked in front of a white, colonial mansion. Steve saw that only the right side of the building had its lights turned on.

"That's the side occupied by the Chariots, our hockey team," Kenneth explained. "They sleep, eat, play games, and watch television there. When they're not playing hockey, that is," he added, grinning.

As Mike drove off with the car, Kenneth, Mark, and Steve walked up to the large front door. Kenneth rapped the brass knocker against the panel and a moment later the door was opened by a tall, middle-aged man whose head was as bald and shiny as a peeled egg.

"Master Kenneth!" he greeted jovially. "We've been expecting you! Hello, Mark!"

"Hello, Andrew," Kenneth and Mark both said. "This is our new member, Steve Crandall," Kenneth went on. "Are his quarters all set up, Andrew?"

"Oh, you bet, sir," replied Andrew, smiling. Steve stared at him, then at "Master Kenneth." My quarters all set up? I can't believe this! Steve thought. Kenneth had reneged on his word from the very beginning! He had said he wouldn't take me with him unless I agreed to go. Well, I *haven't* agreed!

Steve's heart pounded as he saw Andrew extending a hand out to him. "Glad to meet you, Steve," Andrew was saying. "I'm sure you'll enjoy it very much here. Come in, come in. Here, let me take your bag."

"It's just my hockey uniform and skates," Steve explained, automatically handing it to him.

Andrew's gray eyes danced. "I know. It usually is, my boy."

Kenneth chuckled. "Andrew's quite an amusing fellow," he said. "You'll find that he's a lot of fun around here."

I wonder, Steve thought, feeling his skin prickle. He followed Andrew up a spiral staircase and through a door that opened into a large room equipped with several cots. Five, Steve counted, as he thought: cots? I've never slept on a cot in my life! Next to each cot was a chair, a desk, and a desk lamp. Pictures, which covered the peach-painted walls, ranged from astronauts on the moon to hockey players on ice.

"Your cot is number five, Steve," said Andrew, placing the bag on it. "I'll leave you in Mark's custody now. He'll tell you what to do. Good night."

"Good night," Steve heard himself say. He watched Andrew leave and saw Mark standing at the side of the doorway. "What is this, Mark?" he asked. "Everybody seems to think I'm really going to stay here."

"Well, no one is sure of that yet, of course," Mark replied, coming closer. "But we're going to try our best. You're a fine hockey player, Steve, and you might as well face it. Kenneth is going to do everything he can to make you *want* to stay here and play with the Chariots. Well, almost everything," he added, smiling. "A private room, for example. Nobody has one here, except Kenneth. Anyway, he just started the team this year and has already made it the best professional kid's hockey team in the country."

Steve frowned. "Professional?"

"That's right. Professional. We schedule games with the best teams and demand a certain fee. Sometimes we get it, sometimes we don't. But it's always substantial, enough for Kenneth to keep putting money into each of our trust funds as he promised."

"Is he really the head of the Chariots, or is he working for someone else? His father, say."

"Well, he's co-owner with his father," said Mark. "But he runs the Chariots. He's the brains. And he's got them, believe me. Would you believe he's already graduated from college?"

Steve's eyebrows arched. "But he can't be more than thirteen!" he said, incredulous.

"He isn't. But he's brilliant. What's more, he knows as much about hockey as he does math, which he majored in. I'm telling you, Steve, every guy here is really honored by having been picked to play for the Chariots. Not one of them has ever been sorry. I'll warn you: he'll work you hard. You're going to have to practice your tail off, but it'll pay off, because you'll find that you're playing on the best kid's hockey team in the country with good possibilities of joining a professional hockey team in three or four years. Can you think of anything that is more promising than that for kids our age? I'm telling you, I can't."

"I still don't like this," Steve insisted, dropping hard on one of the cots, clamping his hands into fists. "I still feel like I've been kidnapped."

"Steve." Mark came toward him, put a hand on Steve's shoulder. "You're wrong. Believe me. You weren't kidnapped. You were just brought here for a chance of a lifetime to show your ability. You don't think Kenneth's father would let Kenneth get away with a dangerous thing like kidnapping do you?"

I don't know, Steve wanted to say. I don't know Kenneth's father.

"What does his father do?" Steve asked.

"Mr. Agard is president of the Blue Gills hockey team. It's Kenneth's hope that some of us will become good enough to play on it when we're too old to play with the Chariots."

"When is 'too old'?"

"When we turn sixteen," Mark answered.

"How old are you, Mark?"

"Fourteen."

"Where are you from?"

"California."

"California?" Steve frowned. "How long have you been here?"

"Almost a year. I'm a charter member." Mark rubbed his palms together and smiled. "Well, we've shot the breeze long enough. Come on downstairs and I'll introduce you to the guys."

Steve met them all, including the two players with

whom, Mark told him, he was going to be teamed up on Line One: Hal Spoon and Nick Troy. Providing he decided to stay, Mark added as an afterthought.

Steve noticed a large desk to the right of the door as one entered the room, and the big broad-shouldered man who sat behind it. Another man was sitting on a settee, reading a newspaper. Both men seemed preoccupied, yet Steve had a feeling that neither one of them was missing a thing that went on in the room.

Curfew was at ten o'clock, when the lights dimmed, some of them turning off completely.

Back in the room upstairs Steve saw that both Hal Spoon and Nick Troy were his roommates. The other two were Mark Slate and Ray Hutchings. Steve was glad Mark was a roommate, too, mainly because Mark was the only one among the guys Steve knew. Maybe after he got acquainted with some of the other guys he could gain the confidence of at least one of them and find out the *real* story behind all this. Had all these guys been duped to come here as he had been? he wondered. Could be. Not one of them looked happy. Everyone he'd seen so far looked as if he were in a world of his own. What kind of hold had Kenneth Agard, Jr., on them, anyway?

"Your locker's number five, Steve," Mark said as he sat down and started to remove his shoes. "You'll find your 'jamas in there, plus a new outfit of clothes."

Steve looked at him surprised. "New outfit of clothes?" he echoed. "Suppose they don't fit?"

"If they don't, we'll get you ones that will." Mark smiled. "Sleep tight, Steve. Classes are from nine to twelve, then we'll have a hockey scrimmage in the afternoon. So you'll want a good rest. Good night."

"Good night," Steve replied, staring at Mark as if he were already dreaming as he crawled into bed.

## 4

**S**teve and his roommates were awakened at seven o'clock by a soft tapping on the door. He showered, then dressed in his new clothes, finding them to fit him almost perfectly. How did Kenneth Agard, Jr., do it? he wondered. Did he get my measurements from Mom and Dad?

Breakfast was at seven-thirty in the cafeteria next to the recreation room, but Steve didn't feel hungry. He missed home. He missed his mother and father. He finally forced down a biscuit and half a glass of milk.

Steve noticed again the two men he had seen last night. They were standing near the door, talking to each other, apparently oblivious of the twenty-five boys sitting at the three long tables. Yet Steve suspected that there wasn't a thing going on in the room that escaped their attention.

They are probably here to maintain order, he thought. Why else would they be here?

The boys had a break between eight and nine o'clock. At ten minutes of nine a buzzer sounded and the boys got up and started to leave. Steve stared curiously after them until Mark, who had been sitting with him, Hal, and Nick, said "Stay here, Steve. We're going after our workbooks. I'll get yours."

"Okay."

In a few minutes the boys returned, each carrying a workbook and pencil. Mark handed Steve his. "Here you are," he said. "This is all we get, so just listen carefully to your instructor and do as he says. We're put in classes according to our ages. You're thirteen, so you're in Group A. See you at noon."

Steve nodded, feeling slightly numb from the quick pace of things.

"Come on, Steve," said Hal. "I'm in Group A, too."

Steve followed him across the room and sat at the table in front of which a sign on the wall read: GROUP A. Altogether six boys made up the group indicating that there were more fourteen-and fifteen-year-old kids than thirteen-year-olds.

Group A's instructor was Roger Harlan, one of the men Steve had seen in the building. Mr. Harlan, six foot four, dark-haired, built like a football tackle, exchanged introductions with Steve, then took a minute to explain about the subjects.

"We have three one-hour classes each day," he said. "English, math, and social sciences are taught on Mondays, Wednesdays, and Fridays; earth sciences, lab, and Spanish on Tuesdays and Thursdays."

"I don't care about that," Steve said, looking directly into Mr. Harlan's dark brown eyes. "I'm only here for the day."

Harlan smiled. Steve cringed. The smile reminded him of a cobra he had seen once at a zoo. Mr. Harlan went on as if he hadn't heard a word Steve said. "We don't use books, only those workbooks in which you take notes. I suggest you keep your eyes and ears open and write only those parts of my lectures which you think are important."

Steve glanced behind him, wondering if Kenneth might have come into the room. *If he thinks he's*

31

*going to keep me here longer than one day, he's crazy,* Steve thought. But Kenneth wasn't anywhere to be seen. Finally Mr. Harlan's droning ended. Steve picked up his books and followed Mark and the other boys to the classrooms.

After classes were over, Hal asked him, "Well? How do you like our school?"

"I don't," Steve answered. "I want out . . . *now.*"

"Why don't you wait till you skate on our rink and get a feel of our kind of hockey?" a voice cut in at his elbow. "You might change your mind."

Steve looked around at Mark. "I doubt it," he said. But the thought of getting into a hockey uniform and onto the rink intrigued him. What do the Chariots have that I haven't seen before? he wondered. Maybe he could wait at least long enough to find out, he thought, *then* see Kenneth and lay it on the line that he definitely wanted out. And make his decision stick.

The boys rested for an hour after dinner, then got into their hockey uniforms and rode a bus five miles to the coliseum in the city where, Mark explained, the Blue Gills played their local hockey games.

Here, also, the Chariots practiced and played their games.

Steve couldn't help but be impressed by the oval building and the banners that hung from the ceiling, each with the name of a professional hockey team printed on it. The rink was milk-white, the blue and red lines on the ice were like brand-new, bright ribbons.

The players removed the protective rubber from their skates and got on the ice, each one with a hockey stick. Kenneth Agard, Jr., sat in the area reserved for the scorekeeper and reporters, and watched the players skate around the rink for about five minutes before barking his first order.

"All right. We're going to begin scrimmage. Here are the players for Line One defending the goal to my right. Put on white jerseys as I call your names. Goalie, Jason Moore; right defense, Ray Hutchings; left defense, Mark Slate; center, Steve Crandall; right wingman, Hal Spoon; left wingman, Nick Troy. Line Two — no uniform change for you guys. Goalie, Chick Culligan; right defense, Andy Messenger; left defense, Tony Morris; center, Jack

Potter; right wingman, Mel Hale; left wingman, Harvey Malone. All other players please leave the ice."

Steve, his heart pounding after he got his jersey from the pile on the bench, skated to the face-off circle and waited for his opponent, Jack Potter, to get in position in front of him. Jack was a couple of inches taller than he, and few pounds heavier, but Steve dismissed the difference in their sizes. He was in his element now. This was hockey, and an opponent's size didn't matter. He could be a giant as far as Steve was concerned. *This is my game and I'm going to play it to the hilt,* Steve thought.

The referee — a tall, bald-headed man Steve had seen in the recreation hall — blew his whistle, then dropped the puck. Steve and Jack struck at it simultaneously, moving the disk in short, snappy jerks every which way until a hard thrust by Steve sent it scurrying across the ice. Hal got it, stickhandled it toward the goal, then passed it to Nick. Instantly both of Line Two's defensemen charged at Nick. One of them bodychecked him hard just as he passed the puck toward Steve.

Jack sped past Steve, his stick held out in front of him. Quickly Steve dug his skates into the ice and swung in front of Jack, his stick hitting Jack's away then grabbing the puck. He hooked it smoothly, stealing it completely from his opponent, and drawing a surprised and angry look from him.

As Steve stickhandled the puck he looked for an opening behind the crunching goalie, saw one, and shot. *Slap!* The goalie jerked up his right arm in an effort to stop the puck, but missed it by a mile. Goal!

"Nice shooting, Steve!" Kenneth yelled.

Mark skated up beside him. "Beautiful flip-shot, Steve," he said, smiling.

"Thanks," said Steve, smiling back. *This is even easier than I thought, Mark, ol' buddy,* he wanted to say.

As Steve returned to the face-off circle he saw that Jack Potter wasn't as appreciative. Jack's eyes were cold, his jaw set.

The whistle shrilled; the puck dropped. Both centers' sticks cracked like whips as the boys fought for control of the puck. Suddenly Jack spun on both skates, knocking Steve aside, and took possession. Steve stared, surprised, as Jack took off down the ice with the puck, then passed it to a teammate.

Not wasting another second, Steve, anger flushing

his cheeks, bolted down the ice. Quickly he saw a play in the making: Mel Hale, Line Two's right wingman, was wide open near the side of the rink and Jack was skating down center ice. Mel seemed to be the logical player to pass to.

Steve headed for him. A second later Jack passed the puck to Mel. Steve, skating with all the speed he could muster, reached out his stick, grabbed the puck, stopped, then shot it across the ice to Roy. The defenseman caught it, controlled it until his teammates had crossed the blue line, then fired it to Nick. In a wild scramble Nick lost it to Jack who again raced with it to the side of the rink, then down along the boards toward his goal.

Steve, hot on his heels, got near enough to Jack to reach for the puck. This time Jack shot it toward the goal, swinging the stick hard and carelessly. Steve winced as it struck him on the side. He was sure that Jack had done it on purpose, but he controlled his temper.

He started to sprint down the ice but had hardly taken two steps when Jack, glancing over his shoulder, bolted in front of him. Their skates collided. Steve, unable to hold his balance, fell.

A corner of Jack's mouth curved into a grin as he yanked his skate free from Steve's and bolted away. Steve scrambled to his feet, anger boiling inside of him. He'd be darned if he'd let Jack get away with that!

He sprinted across the ice where Harvey, Roy, and Jack were fighting for control of the puck. Suddenly Jack yanked it free and started to stickhandle it down the ice toward his goal. He didn't see Steve coming after him until the very last instant when he suddenly swerved, carrying the puck with him. Steve, seeing an opportunity for a good bodycheck, charged into the tall center. Steve felt the impact of his body striking Jack's. Then both of them slid across the ice. Jack swinging his stick around as an angry snarl tore from him. Not sure whether the center intended to strike him with it or not, Steve didn't take any chances. He grabbed Jack's arm and held it for a moment before he let it go, quite certain by then that Jack wouldn't use it against him.

Jack didn't. But the grim look on his face was unmistakable.

"Okay!" Kenneth yelled. "Line One, off the ice! Give Line Three your jerseys!"

As Steve pulled off his jersey and skated off the ice, he glanced at Kenneth Agard, Jr., and saw a whimsical smile come over the young coach's face.

"Well, how does it feel?" Kenneth said. "Great, right?"

"I guess." Steve took a deep breath, and exhaled it. "Can I see you a minute? It's . . . it's important."

"Not now, Steve. I'm busy now — you can see that." Kenneth turned his attention back to the practice game and immediately started to yell to Line Three, "Get moving, you guys! Get moving!"

He's brushing me off, Steve thought. But I'm going to tell him what's on my mind. He's not going to brush me off for long.

# 5

**T**he team scrimmaged for an hour, then showered and rode back to their quarters, tired and hungry.

Mark, sitting with Steve in the bus as it breezed along smoothly on the winding country road, broke the awkward silence between them. "You really looked good, Steve," he said. "Kenneth was quite impressed."

"I saw that he was," said Steve, remembering his smile.

Hal Spoon looked back at them from the seat ahead and grinned, the first time that Steve remembered seeing anything else on Hal's long slender face besides a sad somber look. "I think that you showed Jack up, too," he said. "You looked great."

"Thanks, Hal," replied Steve. "But I just didn't

want to let him get away with what he was doing, that's all."

Hal's grin broadened. "I figured that," he said, and turned back around.

Steve rested his head back against the seat and closed his eyes. Almost instantly his mother and father came into his thoughts, and a loneliness hit him. He had never been away from them for more than a couple of days. Nor had there ever been more than twenty miles separating them. Now he was in another state and there were over five or six hundred miles between them.

He opened his eyes. "Mark."

"Yeah?"

"I haven't had a chance to tell Kenneth that I don't want to stay. Would you try to see him for me?"

Mark looked at him. "You've been with us just a little while, Steve," he said. "Give yourself more time to think about it."

"I don't need more time," Steve answered. "I want to go home, Mark."

Mark rested his head back, said nothing.

"You heard me, didn't you, Mark?" said Steve. "I said I want to go home."

"Yes, I heard you," Mark said.

"Well?"

"You can't go back, Steve. Not right away."

Steve sat up. "Who's going to stop me? If I want to go back I'll *go* back. Neither you, Kenneth, nor anyone else is going to stop me."

"Sorry, Steve," said Mark calmly. "But you are *not* going back. You might as well face up to that fact now."

Steve's face paled. "You mean that I — I'm like a prisoner?"

Mark shook his head. "It's not like that at all, Steve. It's just that once Kenneth gets a kid he thinks is really a top-notch hockey player, he's going to keep him. And he thinks you're top-notch, Steve. I know he won't want to let you go."

"That's crazy!" Steve cried. "Who does he think he is, anyway?"

"Calm down, Steve. Everyone's staring."

"Let them stare. Just because they're all dumb enough to stay here . . ."

"Sssh!" said Hal, turning to look back at Steve. "The driver's got his eyes on you."

Steve glanced at the rearview mirror and saw the

hard, staring eyes of the driver fixed on him. His heart pounded as he fell back against the seat and stared at the ceiling of the bus.

I must be having a nightmare, he thought. This can't really be happening.

Steve looked for Kenneth during dinnertime, but the young team co-owner and coach was nowhere around. He didn't sit down to eat with the team, anyway, Steve learned. He sat in another part of the house with his parents.

What kind of parents does he have to let him practically have the run of the place? Steve wondered. And what kind of kid was Kenneth, really? Brilliant, yes. And an expert in hockey. But he was more than that. He was a *monster.*

"I'd like to write a letter to my parents," Steve said to Mark after dinner. "Can I have some stationery?"

Mark shook his head. "Sorry, Steve. Nobody writes any letters here."

Steve couldn't believe it. "Why not? Don't you think that our parents want to know what we're doing?"

"Kenneth keeps them in touch," he said. "Don't worry. If anything happens back home, you'll know about it right away. And if anything happens to you, your parents will be notified."

"Why can't *we* write to our parents?" Steve insisted.

"Kenneth believes that by not writing letters the guys won't get homesick," Mark answered. "And it's proven true. I've been here almost a year now and I haven't been homesick at all. You'll get used to it after a while. All the guys feel the same way."

"Well, I don't," said Steve harshly. "I love my parents, and I think they'd want to hear from me."

"They don't expect to," said Mark. "Kenneth explained it to them, and they were agreeable. Honestly, Steve," Mark added, smiling that warm, genial smile of his, "what practical purpose would there be writing letters to your parents? You'd just think about them more, and get homesick. Your playing might suffer, too. Think about it, Steve. There is no organization for young hockey players in the country that is run so expertly and successfully as this one. It's a professional farm team. The big leagues have them, but their players are older than we are, and are in leagues. We aren't. Our games are exhibitions, and we fly all over the country to play the best teams that could be put up against us." His eyes danced. "Know what? Kenneth is considering scheduling games with some of the European countries."

"I can't believe it," said Steve.

"Well believe it," Mark said, his eyes sparkling. "I tell you, that kid's a genius."

"He's a monster," Steve said softly.

Mark chuckled. "That's what I thought, too, when he brought me here," he said. "But I've changed my tune. You might as well change yours, too, Steve. It won't do you any good to fight Kenneth."

"I can try running away."

Mark looked at him. "Steve, what do your parents do?"

"My father — he's a technician in a hospital."

"How much does he earn?"

"I don't know." Steve looked hard at Mark. "Never mind. I know what you're trying to say. We can use the extra money."

Mark smiled. "Right. Come on. Let's take in tonight's video. It's an oldie. A cowboy picture."

Reluctantly, Steve followed Mark upstairs into a room where the videos were shown. Several boys were already there, waiting for the movie to start.

Others kept dribbling in until, promptly at seven-thirty, the movie started.

It turned out to be one that Steve had not seen before. But throughout the picture his mind reverted to his mother and father. It just didn't seem possible, he thought, that they would agree with Kenneth Agard, Jr., about not writing to, or receiving letters from, their son.

**6**

**E**arly on Wednesday morning the team rode by bus
to the airport and jet-lined to Philadelphia. They
were accompanied by their young coach, Kenneth
Agard, Jr., and two chaperones, Mr. Healy and Mr.
Karpis, who were grim-faced, hard-looking men.
Steve wanted desperately to talk to Kenneth, but he
didn't dare. Not with Mr. Healy and Mr. Karpis
around.

They played that evening in the same rink where
the Flyers played. Steve, skating around it during
the pre-game warm up, looked with nervousness
and surprise at the fans streaming in through the en-
tranceways. Never before had he played in front of a
crowd as large as this one was going to be.

The Angels' white satin uniforms, trimmed in

light blue, were a sharp contrast to the Chariots' red ones. Steve didn't know much about the Angels except that they were good. Kenneth would not have scheduled a game with them if they weren't, that's for sure.

At seven-twenty the whistle blew, signaling the players to get off the ice. At seven-twenty-five it blew again, signaling the first lines of both teams to get back on it. The crowd cheered. An announcer named all positions and more cheers went up.

"The game will be divided into three periods of eighteen minutes each," the announcer explained. "Each line will play two minutes three times a period. There will be a ten-minute break in between periods."

In the center face-off circle Steve found himself facing a fair-skinned, brown-eyed boy about his height and slightly thinner. The boy's name was Dick Wirtz. Steve thought: *This is going to be like taking candy from a kid.*

The puck dropped. The whistle shrilled. Sticks clashed as both centers tried to get control of the puck. Suddenly both sticks hooked together and

Steve discovered the powerful strength of his opponent's hands. For one fraction of a second he glanced up, met Dick's eyes squarely, and saw in them the defiance and aggressiveness of a fearless hockey player. Steve's first impression of Dick Wirtz had changed. He had a feeling that if Dick was like this, so were most of the other Angels.

Their sticks broke loose and Dick whacked the puck driving it toward center ice. An Angels' wingman caught the pass and carried it across the Chariots' blue line, his skates biting into the ice as he raced across it. Steve sprinted after him, heading directly toward the Chariots' goal where Jason Moore crouched in the crease, his eyes like black holes in his white mask.

The Angels' wingman tried a slap shot as he sped toward the net. The puck headed for the corner next to Jason's left foot, but the goalie stopped it with his stick and shoved it to Mark Slate as the defenseman skated up beside him.

"Nice save, Jason," said Mark who, Steve had noticed, always had a good word for every guy on the team. He was a regular one-man cheerleading squad.

Mark stickhandled the disk around the back of the net, then passed it to Steve who carried it up along the boards. An Angels' defenseman came pell-mell after him, fierce determination shining in his eyes. Just as Steve shot a pass across the ice toward Nick, the defenseman struck the Chariots' center, checking him into the boards.

*Shreeeek!*

"Boarding!" called the referee, and the game was stopped as the penalized Angel skated off the ice.

During the minute that the Angel sat in the penalty box the Chariots played their hearts out to score. Twice Steve took shots at the Angels' net, only to have the Angels' goalie catch the puck in his gloved hands both times.

It was after the penalized player returned to the ice that a scoring play seemed to be in the making for the Angels. Dick Wirtz had the puck in his possession, stickhandling it down the middle of the ice with his wingmen on either side of him. Roy and Mark stopped in front of their net, helping Jason defend it. From the wings came Hal and Nick, and coming up behind Dick was Steve.

"Take the wingmen!" Steve shouted.

Both Hal and Nick glanced at him with puzzled looks on their faces.

"Take them!" Steve shouted again.

As he yelled he saw the wingmen look over their shoulders. At the same time he dug his skates into the ice, sprinting around the right wingman in a move so swift that it confused the Angel. As the wingman turned to follow him, Nick checked him, throwing him off-balance and giving Steve the opportunity to go after the puck carrier.

Dick was within eight feet of the goal when he reared his stick back and started to bring it down in a hard slap-shot swing. Skating with all the power he could muster, Steve came abreast of the Angels' center's side and reached out his stick. Just as Dick's stick came down in a sweeping arc, Steve grabbed the puck, swept around in an ice-flying circle, and headed back in the opposite direction. A roar burst from the fans as he stickhandled the puck down the ice, not an Angel in front of him except the goaltender.

Skating across center ice and then over the blue

line into Angels' territory, he looked at the net for a target. The goalie was crouched in front of it, covering the middle, gloved hand and stick ready.

Steve headed for him, the sound of fast-approaching, singing blades behind him. When he was almost four feet from the crease, Steve changed the position of his hands on the stick, swung to the left, and shot. Whack! The puck skittered through the hole between the goalie's out-swinging stick and the edge of the net.

Goal! Thunder boomed from the fans. Sticks clattered against the boards as the Chariots expressed their approval.

"Nice shot, Steve!" Mark said as he and the other members of the Chariots' line swarmed around him.

Steve skated slowly toward the neutral zone, breathing tiredly. As he wiped at the sweat that drizzled down his face someone brushed hard against his elbow. He looked at the player. It was Dick Wirtz.

Steve ignored him.

Face-off. The puck dropped, the whistle blew, and Dick's stick was a fraction of a second ahead of

Steve's at the puck. The disk shot across the ice to an Angels' wingman who carried it toward center ice. Steve, swinging around to go after the puck, felt his skate being hooked by the blade of another skate. As if someone had yanked his leg from under him, he fell. A chuckle rippled from the offender, Dick Wirtz, and Steve saw the center skate past him.

But no whistle blew. The ref hadn't seen Dick pull the violation.

Steve scrambled to his feet and took off down the middle of the ice, anger rising in him. He wasn't looking for revenge though. He was looking for the puck.

Suddenly a horn buzzed. The first two minutes were up. The lines of both teams skated off the ice. Their second lines skated on.

Steve was bushed as he sat down. He took the towel handed to him by one of the guys, wiped his face with it, then passed it to the next player.

In a little while he felt better. His heart stopped pounding. The cool air of the huge room freshened his face.

He looked at the crowd. The place was jam-packed.

Chick Culligan, the Chariots' Line Two goalie, had three saves within the first minute, then missed a high-flying shot for the Angels' first score. Chariots 1, Angels 1.

The Angels' Line Three garnered another score to go into the lead 2 to 1.

"Let's get 'em," said Mark as the buzzer sounded and Line One scrambled back on the ice.

Refreshed from the rest, Steve felt more comfortable and less nervous now than the first time he was on the ice. Within seconds he stole the puck from an Angels' wingman and was moving it down toward center ice. As he crossed the red line he saw a blue-uniformed player creeping up on him at his left side. Steve knew that a body-check was ready to come. But he wasn't about to accept it.

Stopping almost on the spot and hooking the blade of his stick around the puck, he saw the player whisk by him. It was Dick Wirtz. Dick reached his stick out to grab the puck, but caught Steve's stick instead. A quick, sudden yank, catching Steve by surprise, pulled the stick out of Steve's hand and flung it across the ice.

Mouth opened as he stared at Dick, Steve felt a moment of intense embarrassment. Never had anyone ever yanked a hockey stick out of his hand before.

# 7

**H**is face red, Steve bolted after the stick and scooped it off the ice. He glanced around and saw that Dick still had control of the puck and was carrying it up the ice toward the Chariots' goal.

"That-a-way, kid! Don't let him get away with it!" a fan shouted, then laughed hilariously.

*Very funny,* thought Steve as he shot across the red line into Chariots' territory.

Dick crossed the blue line and shot a pass to a wingman as Mark sped up to him and checked him hard with his hip. Dick swung his stick around as he spun to keep his balance, and almost hit Steve. The loose puck skidded toward the boards, and Steve skated after it. He, Mark, and an Angels' defenseman reached it at the same time.

Mark jammed the man against the boards, holding

55

him there until Steve got the puck. As Steve turned he saw Dick bolting toward him, eyes flashing anger.

With a snap of his stick Steve passed the puck to Hal, and Hal stickhandled it across center ice with no one near him. Steve crouched and dug his skates hard in swift pursuit, then crashed to the ice as Dick's skate rammed into one of his. Stunned, Steve slid across the ice, colliding into Roy and knocking him off balance.

Hal got within four feet of the net and shot. The puck never got past the crease as the Angels' goaltender stopped it with his glove.

Neither line scored. And, after each line completed its third session on the ice, Steve was glad that break-time had come. The score was still 2 to 1 in the Angels' favor.

As both teams headed to their respective locker rooms, someone touched Steve's arm. Steve glanced around. It was Hal.

"I'd like to talk to you, Steve," Hal said in a low voice.

Steve frowned, "About what?"

"About —" Hal's eyes suddenly focused on someone beyond Steve, and he hesitated. "Later," he said.

Steve looked over his left shoulder and saw Mark behind him. What was Hal going to say, he thought, that he didn't want Mark to hear?

They sat on benches in the locker room, their helmets on the floor between their feet. Steve looked across the room at Hal, but the wingman was resting back against a locker, his eyes closed.

Standing near the door were the two men who had accompanied the team, Mr. Healy and Mr. Karpis. They weren't just chaperones, Steve thought. They were *guards*. He and the rest of the team were their prisoners.

Kenneth Agard, Jr., entered the room with a smile and a basketful of oranges.

"Good game so far, men," he said, his eyes partially hidden behind his glasses. His smile faded slightly. "But you've got to do better. Only one goal in the first period is ridiculous."

He gave them each an orange, which they peeled and ate. When Steve glanced again at Hal he met Hal's eyes. He was sure they were trying to tell him something.

A few minutes later, when the teams were back on the ice for a brief warm up before the second period, Steve glided up beside Hal.

"What did you want to say to me, Hal?" he asked softly.

"Never mind," said Hal. His eyes darted nervously around the rink.

"But you said you wanted to talk to me."

Hal's face darkened. "I changed my mind," he said stiffly. "Quit bugging me, okay?"

Steve looked at him, puzzled, then skated away. A couple of minutes later the buzzer sounded. The second period was ready to begin.

Hal's got something on his mind, Steve thought. I wish he'd tell me what it is.

Face-off. This time Steve grabbed the puck, then almost tripped over Dick's right skate. He caught his balance and saw Hal grab the puck and pass it to Nick. Nick raced with it across the blue line into the neutral zone, then passed it to Mark. A whistle shrilled, and Steve saw that Mark had had his left foot behind the Chariots' blue line when Hal had passed the puck to him, an off-side violation.

Face-off between Nick and an Angels' forward.

The forward grabbed the puck and passed it to Dick, who headed down the middle of the ice. In a second Steve was hot on his tail. Oblivious of the fast approaching center, Dick seemed to be ignoring his wingman as he raced toward the goal.

Steve put on an extra burst of speed, caught up to Dick, and checked him with his hip. The blow knocked Dick off balance; made him lose control of the puck. Grabbing the disk with the blade of his stick, Steve turned and headed back up the ice. As both of the Angels' wingmen tore after him, he passed the puck to Mark. Mark stickhandled it toward the neutral zone and across the blue line. Blocked by a defenseman, Mark brought himself up short, ice spraying from his skates. For an instant he stood there, his stick guarding the puck as he looked around quickly for someone to pass to. Sweat shone on his face.

Dick came up unexpectedly behind him, checked the Chariots' defenseman on the left hip, and knocked him to the ice. Then Dick grabbed the puck, but Steve, bolting by him, hit his stick, stole the puck, and in the same swift motion shot it toward the net. The surprised goalie, caught off-guard, saw the puck flying across the ice toward him too late to be able to stop it.

Goal! Chariots 2, Angels 2.

Steve, skating slowly back toward the center circle as the Chariots' bench thundered their approval of his shot and of the score, cut toward Hal and said, "Hal! Are you going to tell me what you wanted to see me about?"

"No!" Hal answered. "Forget it, will you?"

Steve frowned, then skated to the face-off circle. I wonder what he wanted to tell me, Steve thought, and why he's changed his mind. Is he afraid somebody else might know what he wanted to say? But who? Mark? Was Hal afraid that Mark might then tell Kenneth whatever it was he wanted to say?

Again Steve grabbed the face-off. Seconds later he saw Hal carrying the puck down center ice, no one near him except an Angels' defenseman. Hal evaded him easily, bolted straight for the net, then cut sharply to the right. Steve watched expectantly.

"Shoot, Hal! Shoot!" he cried.

Steve had barely gotten the words out of his mouth when Hal shot. The puck streaked past the

Angels' goalie's right foot into the net. It was 3 to 2, the Chariots' favor.

"Good shot, Hal!" Steve shouted. Well, whatever was on Hal's mind, it wasn't affecting his playing, thought Steve.

Hal just grinned.

The buzzer sounded. The next lines took over. At 9:12 Mel Hale powdered a ten-foot shot into the net to put the Chariots ahead, 4 to 2. Line Three kept up the hot scoring streak as right winger Ray Van-Sickle peppered in the fifth score.

As Line One returned to the ice for their last chance that second period, Steve expected some hard checking from the Angels, and got it. The clock read 5:19 when he stickhandled the puck across center ice, determined to sock in his third goal and earn himself a hat trick.

But Dick Wirtz seemed equally determined that Steve would not get what he wanted. Just over the blue line the Angels' center checked Steve with a hip blow that rocked the Chariots' center so hard his head swam. Not only did Steve lose control of the puck, but he lost his balance, too. He went down, hitting the ice and skidding across it for ten feet.

By the time Steve regained his balance, Dick had the puck and was stickhandling it toward center ice. Steve, struggling back to his feet, saw Mark and Hal skate after Dick. Both were fearless skaters. Steve was sure that if the entire line joined in an attack against them, neither would give an inch.

Dick made the mistake of trying to shoot the puck between them. Realizing what he intended to do, both players got in front of him like a human wall. The puck struck Mark's left skate and ricocheted toward the boards. At the same time Dick plowed into him and Hal, and it was only because Mark put his arms around Dick that none of them lost his balance and fell.

I'll never understand Mark as long as I keep playing with the Chariots, Steve thought. Even on the ice he doesn't forget that he's a gentlemen.

An Angels' defenseman grabbed the puck off the boards and passed it to a teammate. During the next few moments of hard offensive playing, the Angels got the puck into Chariots' territory. And, as the clock ticked off 4:11, an Angels' defenseman found a target in the Chariots' net and hit it. Goalie Jason missed it by a mile.

Chariots 5, Angels 3.

None of the next two lines managed to score before the second period ended.

Steve was glad that there was only one more period to go. He was bushed. He removed his helmet and joined the rest of the team as it headed for the locker room. Again the coach, Kenneth Agard, Jr., came in with a pleased smile and a basketful of oranges.

"Gang, nice work!" he said proudly. "I knew you could do it! Here, an orange apiece. After the game we're going to stop at a restaurant for a real meal. Steak. How does that suit you?"

A shout of approval rose from the players.

It was while they were eating the oranges that Steve noticed one of the chaperones, Mr. Healy, was not in the room. He thought little about it until a few moments later when he looked around for Hal.

Hal wasn't in the room either.

**8**

The third period started with Don Steuben, a sub, playing on Line One in place of Hal.

Where was Hal, anyway? Steve wondered, looking around and not seeing him. Was he sick? Or in trouble? From the way he'd been acting lately *something* was bothering him, Steve thought.

Then he saw Mr. Healy hurrying down the aisle, an anxious look on his stonelike face, and stopping to talk to Kenneth. They both looked excited, concerned. I bet it's about Hal, Steve thought. He's probably run away. Maybe that's what he wanted to see me about, to ask me if I'd run away with him.

The thought frightened Steve. He remembered the discussion he had with Mark about leaving the Chariots, leaving Kenneth, and getting the response that it was impossible. How do you like that? Steve thought as the impact of the situation hit him even harder. We really *are* Kenneth's prisoners, and can't do a thing about it! Not one thing! Who can blame Hal for running away?

Steve couldn't get the awful thought out of his mind, and twice during the first few moments he found himself bodychecked so hard that his legs were knocked from underneath him.

"C'mon, Steve!" Mark said to him. "Get with it!"

Gradually his concern, that he was one of Kenneth's unwilling players, was taken over by his natural abilities as a better-than-average hockey player, and in seconds he was back in the midst of all the action again. Three times he took shots at the goal, and all three times the Angels' goalie made a save. But Steve was in there fighting, and when the two minutes were up he was breathing tiredly and perspiring freely.

Fifteen seconds after Line Two took to the ice, Mel Hale was sent to the penalty box for high sticking, and for the next few seconds the Angels made a strong attempt to take advantage of the four-man team. A wild shot just missed the edge of the net and went flying against the boards. Jack Potter, the

Chariots' red-headed, scrappy Line Two center, took the puck and "ragged" it for the next thirty-five seconds (ragging was keeping the puck to delay the game as long as possible). He stickhandled it down the side of the rink and across the ice, stopping abruptly to evade an Angel, then sprinting forward again, always in control of the puck. Chariot and Angel fans alike cheered as he craftily and successfully eluded his opponents.

At last Mel's penalty time was up; he returned to the ice. But the lines completed their two minutes without scoring.

It was when Line Three took the ice that Steve got a glimpse of Mr. Healy. The stone-faced chaperone was coming on the ice through the gate, pulling Hal Spoon after him. Hal, on his skates, seemed to be coming against his will. But he was coming.

"It doesn't pay to run away," said Mark, sitting next to Steve. "Nobody has ever gotten away with it yet. Hal will be sorry he tried it."

Steve stared at Mark. "Sorry?" he echoed. "Why should he be sorry? Is Kenneth going to hurt him, or something?"

Mark shrugged. For the first time, Mark didn't seem to have an answer.

Line Three failed to change the score, and Line One went back on the ice for the second time that period. Steve wondered if Hal would play, but Hal didn't. Kenneth, Steve saw, was having a "man-to-man" talk with him.

Mark's statement rang in Steve's ears even as the ref dropped the puck for the face-off. *It doesn't pay to run away. Nobody has ever gotten away with it yet.* That meant that others had tried it, too, and failed.

Steve played almost automatically during the two minutes, twice hearing Mark yelling at him, "Let's go, Steve! Let's go!"

He was sure that a combination of hard playing — and luck — was with the Chariots as they left the ice. They had failed to score, but they had kept the Angels from scoring, too.

It wasn't till Line Three's last time on the ice that another goal was made. Chariots' center Chuck Durling, carrying the puck across the Angels' blue line, seemed intent on going all the way. But, just as he neared the goal crease, he circled to the left. Drawing the anxious goalie after him, Chuck passed the puck to the wingman coming up behind him, Ray VanSickle. And Ray, taking advantage of the "deked" goalie (a move drawing the goalie out of position), shot the puck into the net.

Chariots 6, Angels 3.

A minute later the game was over, the Chariots receiving loud applause as they left the rink. One remark Steve heard from a fan was, "Never in my life have I seen a kids' team like those Chariots. They're fantastic!"

Steve had to agree. He knew he should feel proud of the win, and of his own performance. But the realization that he was a hockey "slave" of Kenneth Agard, Jr.'s, scared him. Whether the Chariots were Kenneth's "slaves," or "prisoners," or whatever name fitted, Steve couldn't believe that such a thing existed. How could it be allowed? he wondered. How could Kenneth, a kid no older than he was, get away with keeping guys on the team against their wishes? It was *crazy*.

But he *was* doing it. And he *was* getting away with it.

Steve shook.

At the restaurant, where Kenneth had made reservations, Steve told himself that he would never have eaten the steak, potatoes, and all that sumptuous-tasting salad if he weren't so ravenously hungry.

They stayed at a motel that night. The next morning they bused to the airport and took Flight 617 home. Steve was about to sit with Hal on the plane, when Mark told him that their seating arrangement was the same flying back as it was flying up. Disappointed, Steve rose and went to occupy the seat with Mark.

"I'm sorry, Steve," said Mark. "But it's the rules."

"Kenneth's rules, I suppose," Steve replied, disgruntled.

"He's boss," reminded Mark.

During most of the flight Steve was silent. Only once, out of curiosity, did he break the silence by asking Mark, "You never told me about your parents. What does *your* father do?"

Mark hesitated. "He's an invalid."

"Oh? I'm sorry."

"My mother's a secretary."

"Got any brothers and sisters?"

"One brother, two sisters. I came third."

"I'm the only child in my family," said Steve. "But I guess you know that."

They fell silent again. This time Steve wondered if that brief conversation had gotten Mark thinking about his family, too.

The next day Steve finally had a chance to tell Kenneth that he had had enough and wanted to go home. He found Kenneth in his office, a large room whose walls were covered with book shelves and pictures — mostly hockey pictures. The head of the Chariots hockey team seemed lost behind a huge, oak desk on which were books, papers, pads, and a red telephone.

"Hey, nice game yesterday, Steve!" Kenneth exclaimed. He smiled as he leaned back in his swivel chair, put his elbows on its wide arms and steepled his fingers. "Played like a real pro."

"Thanks," Steve said, feeling good about the praise. "Did the best I could."

"No, you didn't. You could do better." Kenneth chuckled. "And that will come with experience — experience you'll gain the longer you're with us. I've got big plans for you, Steve. *Big* plans." He rocked a couple of times on the chair, then stopped and focused his eyes on Steve. "One of these days you're going to be rich. *Rich*, Steve. Hear me?"

"I don't want to be rich," Steve said, meeting Kenneth's eyes directly. "I want out. Now."

The smile on Kenneth's face faded. A cold, hard look came over it as he glanced away from Steve's direct gaze and sat back in his chair. "You seem to have a short memory, Steve," he said calmly. "You can't get out. We've told you that."

Steve jumped to his feet. "Why not?" he shouted. "Who are you to keep me here a prisoner? I'll run away! I'll call the police!"

Kenneth's eyes turned back to Steve. For the first time since Steve had met Kenneth, Steve had never seen a look in the young co-owner's eyes as he was seeing now. It was the look of a leader — a tyrant — who knew what he wanted and got it, at whatever the cost.

"No, you won't," he said, his voice low, deliberate. "You're not going to do anything — but play hockey."

Steve sat back down, Kenneth's voice hanging like

a whip over him. He had once said to somebody —
to Mark — that Kenneth was a monster. Now he
was sure of it.

"Our discussion is over, Steve," Kenneth said, the
cold glare gone from his eyes, his voice gentle — almost gentle — once again. "See you at breakfast."

Steve got up. "Yeah," he said, and left.

I can't believe this, he thought. What'll I do now?

A week later the Chariots flew to Buffalo for a
game against the Blue Leafs. Steve, his mind made
up that he wasn't going to stay with the Chariots no
matter what Kenneth Agard, Jr., said, started at
face-off with no desire to play. Hal was back after
having been gone a few days, but Steve didn't know
where he'd been, and Hal wasn't talking. He
seemed raring to play, however.

The ref dropped the puck. The Blue Leafs' center, a kid with strong arms and chunky legs, grabbed
the puck easily, and for the entire two-minute session the Chariots might as well have had only four
men on the ice. At 16:42 the Blue Leafs scored.

If I don't play Kenneth will *have* to let me go,
Steve thought.

When Line One got off the ice and Line Two got on it, Kenneth came and sat down beside Steve. If he was angry he didn't show it.

"Steve," he said, "you're not the first kid to act this way. Others have, and later changed their minds. You will be punished, naturally. Firstly, you'll have to skip a meal. Maybe two, or even three, depending on your cooperation. Secondly, you'll be dismissed of all the fun privileges: games, movies, and so on. Thirdly, a check won't go to your parents." He smiled at Steve. "Don't be a child all your life. Grow up. In mind, anyway."

He stood up. "Think about it," he said, and returned to his seat near the gate.

Steve stared after him. A chill rippled up and then down his spine. He had never in his life met a kid like Kenneth Agard, Jr., he thought, and he hoped he never would again.

Line Two tied the score. Then Line Three broke it, only to have it tied again just seconds before they got off the ice.

Chariots 2, Blue Leafs 2.

As Line One started to leave the bench, Kenneth

grabbed Steve by the arm. "I hope you gave it some thought, Steve," he said, smiling. "You're a very good athlete. I hope you're an intelligent one, too."

Steve looked directly into his eyes, but said nothing.

I have done a *lot* of thinking, Kenneth, he wanted to say. But I'm not going to tell you about what.

This time he grabbed the face-off and played as well — if not better — than in the game against the Angels. He was angry, and being angry made him more determined. He socked in a goal during the session, then assisted on another goal in the third session. The game turned out to be a scoring spree for the Chariots. It ended 9 to 3 in their favor. Steve was credited with a hat trick, having scored his third goal in the last period.

"Good game, Steve," Kenneth said, smiling, as the boys streamed off the ice. "I knew you were as intelligent as you were athletic."

Buttering me up, Steve thought. If he only knew what I have in mind.

# 9

The players changed their clothes in the locker room, then were bused to their motel where Kenneth had reserved rooms for them for the night.

At seven o'clock they piled into the motel's dining room and had supper: duckling, mashed potatoes, and salad. A meal fit for a king, thought Steve. But — oh, man — wouldn't I go for a big, fat, juicy hamburger for a change!

Anyway, I still don't want a part of it. We're Kenneth's puppets. He pulls the strings and we jump, Steve reflected solemnly.

Another thing: How do we know that he really sends checks to our parents? We never see the checks. He could be lying. In any case, Mom and Dad lived without the checks before, and they could again.

Steve noticed that both Mr. Healy and Mr. Karpis were sitting near the head of the two tables. No one could possibly leave the room without at least one of the men seeing him.

The team's rooms were on the fourth floor, high enough, Steve realized, to discourage anybody from escaping.

Steve was in a room with three other boys, including Mark Slate. They watched TV till ten o'clock, then Mark clicked it off and turned off the light.

Steve lay in bed, his eyes open, his mind in high gear. He had decided that tonight he'd escape and go to the police — or make a bold attempt at it.

He glanced several times at his wrist watch. There was just enough light shining in through the drape-covered window to be able to read it. At a quarter of twelve he crawled out of bed, taking care not to wake any of the other guys. He dressed, picked up his shoes, and tiptoed to the door. Turning the knob, he opened the door carefully and peered out.

His heart sank as he saw one of the chaperones sitting on a chair down at the end of the hall. Man! Kenneth was really making sure that no one was going to run away!

Steve closed the door quietly and returned to the bed, his hopes of escaping gone down the drain. He lay on the covers for only a few minutes when he thought of the fire escape. Of course! Every motel at least three or four stories high had a fire escape!

He slid out of bed, tiptoed to the window, and peered out. There was a balcony, but no fire escape.

Once again his heart took a nose-dive. Couldn't he be just a bit lucky once?

Then he thought, wasn't there usually a fire escape from a balcony?

Excitement erased his hopeless feeling for a minute as he unlocked the window and groped for hand-grips to open it. He found them. Slowly, silently, he lifted the window, picked up his shoes, and crawled out.

He looked to the side of the balcony, and his heart jumped. There *was* a fire escape!

Quietly he closed the window, climbed over the balcony, stepped onto the fire escape, and started to make the swift, long descent to the dark alley below. A chill wind was blowing. By the time Steve reached the bottom his teeth were chattering.

Suddenly a voice above him cut through the

night. "Steve! Come back here! You'll freeze to death in that cold!"

The voice was hard to recognize in the strong wind, and the face Steve saw peering over the balcony was just a shadowy blur. But he was sure it was Mark's.

Steve put his shoes on and ran. He reached the street and bolted to the right, the wind biting through his clothes. No one was on the street. There were no cars. The only lights were those on the high poles at the end of each block.

He crossed to the next block, ran on. Two men loomed out of the darkness ahead of him, and he turned and hid in the shadows of a building. When they went by he ran on, stumbled off the curb, and fell. He bruised his hands and dirtied his clothes, but he scrambled to his feet and raced on down the street.

Halfway down the block he saw what looked like a telephone booth. Hope flared in him as he sprinted toward it. It *was* a telephone booth! He entered it. His hands trembled as he took off the receiver.

But, how can I call the police? he thought. I haven't got a cent on me! His throat ached.

He heard sharp heels clicking on the sidewalk, and he ducked. Was someone already after him? Had Mark gotten the message to Mr. Healy or Mr. Karpis so quickly that one of them could already be hot on his trail?

But the sound of the footsteps was not familiar. Nor did they have that hurrying sound that they would have if they belonged to someone chasing him.

Steve stood up, and saw a man coming briskly down the sidewalk. He was wearing a topcoat and hat, and had his coat collar turned up around his neck to protect it from the cold wind.

"Mister!" Steve cried, stepping out of the booth. "You got some change I can have to make a phone call?"

The man stopped, startled, and peered at Steve hesitantly from under bushy eyebrows. He was old, Steve saw. In his fifties or sixties. And he was carrying a lunch bag. Probably going to work or going home from work, Steve figured.

He's hesitating because he thinks I'm a street bum, Steve thought. "Please, sir?" he said. "I really would like to make a phone call."

The man's gaze roved over Steve's hair, his clothes, his shoes. Sizing him up, like a man sizing up a car he's considering buying. "Kind of young to be out this late, aren't you?" he snorted. "And without a coat. You'll freeze your ears off."

"That's why I want to make the phone call, sir," Steve said, praying that the man would give him the money and not waste any more time.

"All right," the man said, pushing back his coat and taking some change from his pocket. "And make sure you get home, okay? You're lucky I came around when I did."

"I know, sir," Steve said.

The man handed the change he was holding to Steve. "Here you are," he said.

"Thanks!" Steve cried, accepting the coins. "I appreciate it, sir."

The man pulled his coat about him, gave Steve another quick, stern glance, then went on, his heels clicking on the sidewalk. I guess I can't blame him, Steve thought. I'd feel as he does, too, if I were in his place. Steve re-entered the phone booth, stuck the dimes into the proper slot, then dialed 0. The phone rang. Once . . . twice . . .

He looked up the street. Two men were coming from the direction of the motel! Mr. Healy and Mr. Karpis? Steve's heart pounded.

"Operator," said a calm voice over the receiver.

"Hello! Get me the police! Quick!" Steve cried.

"One moment, please."

Steve could hear the men's feet pounding on the pavement. In a moment they would be crossing the intersection.

"Sergeant Williams speaking," a man's deep voice said into his ear. "Can I help you?"

"Yes!" Steve said. "This is Steve Crandall! I'm with the Chariots hockey team, and I'm . . . I'm in deep trouble!"

"Now take it easy," Sergeant Williams's voice came calmly over the wire. "Just what kind of deep trouble —"

Steve couldn't take another second to explain what kind of trouble he was in. The two men — Mr. Healy and Mr. Karpis — were running across the intersection and would catch him in no time if he didn't hightail it out of there. He dropped the phone and, wrenched with fear, sprinted out of the telephone booth. What would the men do to him if they caught him? Take him back to the motel? Beat him up?

He raced to the end of the block, and was halfway down the next one when one of the men caught up to him and grabbed him by the arm.

"Okay, kid," said Mr. Healy, his breath coming in gasps. "That's enough. Kenneth won't like this one bit. Not one bit."

He started to drag Steve back to the motel and met Mr. Karpis who had just emerged from the telephone booth. Steve's heart sank. Now they knew who he was trying to call!

"Did you find out who he was calling?" Mr. Healy asked.

"No. I just got some operator," Mr. Karpis grunted.

Steve started to breathe a sigh of relief when Mr. Healy grabbed him by the collar. "Did you talk to a cop?" he snapped, glaring at him.

"No! I was trying to get my parents . . . but I didn't have time," Steve answered.

"You'd better be telling the truth, kid," said Healy, and for a moment Steve thought Healy would swat him across the face, but he only grabbed Steve by a wrist and started pulling him down the street, back to the motel. They headed quickly for the elevator before the clerk, sitting at a desk inside a small office, could notice them. They rode up to the fourth floor where Mr. Karpis stopped at Room 431, unlocked the door, and went in. Mr. Healy escorted Steve to Room 433.

"You'll stay in here with me till morning," Mr. Healy commanded, closing the door behind them. His eyes were like hot coals as he looked down at Steve. "I've never beat up a kid, but getting me out in this kind of night sure makes me want to do it to you."

Steve cringed. He was sure Mr. Healy would do it, too. Both he and Mr. Karpis acted like two different men when they had caught him on the street . . . almost like hardened criminals who wouldn't hesitate a second to hurt him.

Mr. Healy shoved Steve toward one of the single beds. "Get out of your clothes and into bed," he ordered. "And hurry. Running away is bad enough without your getting sick, too."

Shivering from a combination of cold and fear, Steve kicked off his shoes, pulled off his clothes, and crawled under the covers. He was angry, but more angry at himself for failing to escape than from what to expect from Kenneth Agard, Jr.

**10**

**S**teve ignored Mark at breakfast and during the entire flight back home, blaming Mark for having "squealed" on him to the two chaperones.

"I'm sorry, Steve," Mark said apologetically. "But I had to do it. Kenneth depends on me. You shouldn't have run away."

Oh, sure, Steve wanted to say, anger steaming up inside him. But he kept silent.

For some reason of his own, Kenneth didn't talk with Steve about Steve's running away until after they were settled back at his home. There, two hours later, Mark came after Steve in the Recreation Room.

"Steve, Kenneth wants to see you," he said.

Silently, Steve followed him out of the room to Kenneth's den. The young mentor of the Chariots hockey team was ensconced in his swivel chair behind the huge, oak desk.

"Hello, Steve," he greeted him pleasantly. "Please sit down."

Steve sat on a plush armchair at the opposite side of the desk. Kenneth nodded to Mark, and Mark left.

"Steve," Kenneth began, picking up a folded sheet of printed matter, "you've seen this before. Remember it?"

Steve's eyes widened. He nodded. "It's the contract you asked me to sign. But I never did."

"Look again, Steve," said Kenneth, pointing at a signature on the second page.

Steve leaned forward, and a rush of anger swept over him. There, on the dotted line, was his name in his own handwriting! And below it, his father's!

"I didn't sign that!" he cried. "And neither did my Dad! Someone forged those signatures!"

Kenneth smiled. "Say what you want to, but it's your signature and your father's, and they bind you to me and to the Chariots. So, no matter what you do, Steve, you will only be hurting yourself. And, of course, the team."

"I don't want to play with you anymore," Steve said flatly. "I want to go home."

"You can't," said Kenneth. "You have an obligation, and you can't back out of it. It's only a waste of time and energy, believe me. You're not the only one who felt misused, or disenchanted, during the first two or three weeks. Others have, too, and tried to run away. Oh, not many. Hal Spoon, as you know. And a couple of others. It took them a while to realize how really childish they were."

He lay the contract back on the desk, got up, and went to the door. "Of course, you'll have to be penalized, Steve," he went on in that same, unruffled tone. "I'm sorry. But I have made strict regulations here, and I must see that everybody abides by them. You'll be under Mr. Healy's attention for the next couple of days."

Mr. Healy was outside of the door, waiting for Steve. He took Steve's arm and led him down the hall to another room. He switched on a light, told Steve to read the instructions that were tacked on the door, and left. Steve tried to turn the knob, but couldn't. He was locked in.

He read the instructions.

1. This will be your quarters for the next 48 hours.
2. Your meal will be brought in to you three times a day.
3. As you see, there is no television for you to watch, no book to read, no paper, or pencil with which to write. You will have nothing to do, although any exercise you do would be to your advantage.
4. There is a button on the desk. Press it if you want any help.

A lump formed in Steve's throat as he looked around him. There was a bed, a chair, a lamp, a desk, and a rectangular mirror hung on one wall. Above the mirror was a round, framed object that looked like a built-in speaker. A door was open, showing a small room with a toilet and sink inside.

I can't believe it! Steve thought. This room is a jail cell! I'm in solitary confinement!

His heart pounding, Steve stepped to the desk and pressed the button that was on the right-hand side of it.

A moment later Kenneth's voice answered through the speaker. "What is it, Steve?"

*What is it, Steve? You would think that everything was hunky-dory!*

"I want to get out of here, that's what!" Steve yelled. "You can't keep me in here!"

"You'll be in there for forty-eight hours, Steve," Kenneth said, not a ruffle in his voice. "Try to do some exercise, and then rest. You might even sleep. You'll find that time goes fastest that way."

"Kenneth, you're a monster!" cried Steve, glaring at the speaker.

He received no reply.

"You hear me? You're a monster!" he shouted, then jumped onto the bed, holding back tears that fought to come.

What could he do? Nothing. He was Kenneth's prisoner.

He got his first meal in half an hour. It was a bowl of cereal, a banana, and a glass of milk. There was nothing wrong with that, he admitted.

He was worried about what his lunch, and his dinner, would be. Would he be given the same meal as he had for breakfast?

Surprisingly, the lunch he received was of the

same high quality as the meals that were served to the team. It was the same with dinner. He had to admit that the meals were more than satisfactory.

But the loneliness of the almost bare room, and the quietness of it, got to him. The only sounds he heard were his own breathing, his footsteps when he walked across the bare floor, and the protesting springs when he lay on the bed. Not a sound came from outside of the room.

That night, as he thought of his mother and father, he wept. Did they really know where he was? he wondered. Did they know that he played with the Chariots? Or had Kenneth really talked with them and gotten their permission to let Steve play hockey with the Chariots? Or had Kenneth lied about the whole thing?

Two days later Kenneth's voice sounded warm and pleasant as it came over the speaker. "Good morning, Steve. I trust you had a good night's sleep."

Steve, sitting on the edge of the bed in his pajamas — at least Kenneth was generous enough to give him those, too — nodded. "I did," he said.

"Good. Can I have your word that you won't pull anything foolish again?"

Steve hesitated.

"Okay. You need not answer that," said Kenneth. "You know what the consequences are, except that the next time your confinement would be for three days. Mr. Healy will be there in a minute to take you to breakfast. Meanwhile, I won't see you till hockey practice this afternoon. You're a good protégé, Steve. Listen to me, and you won't ever be sorry."

Steve told himself that he would never again want to spend time in that cell-like room. But he wasn't going to stay with the Chariots, either.

Somehow he was going to find a way to get away from them, and from the clutches of Kenneth Agard, Jr.

**11**

**S**teve almost cried out with joy when he heard that the Chariots were going to Mulberry City on Saturday to play the Condors. Mulberry City, situated on a lake about one hundred miles north of Water Falls, was where his Uncle Mike lived.

Wouldn't it be great if Uncle Mike read about the Chariots and went to the game? But Steve knew that he might as well wish for a trip to the moon: Uncle Mike didn't give a hoot for hockey.

The team bused to Mulberry City. Even though Mark and Steve sat together, not a word was mentioned about Steve's solitary confinement. Nor did Steve mention a word to Mark about his Uncle Mike's living in Mulberry City.

Maybe — just maybe — I might find a chance to telephone Uncle Mike, Steve thought hopefully.

There was something else about Mulberry City that bolstered his hopes. It had a college with a fine hockey team, and a kid's hockey league that had been spawning a state championship team for the last three years.

A couple of times in the past Steve's mother and father had brought him there to see a game. Wouldn't it be something, he thought, if they came to see this one? Or would Kenneth have informed them about it?

I doubt it, Steve thought. I can't see him letting our parents know about a game every time the Chariots play near their hometown.

Arriving in Mulberry City, the Chariots rode directly to the rink, passing beneath banners that were strung across the streets:

CONDORS vs CHARIOTS
DEC. 2

When the team entered the rink Steve could see that the promotion had really paid off: half of the stadium was already filled, and people were still pouring in.

Playing opposite Steve at center was a boy named

Curt Hilliard. He was shorter than Steve, but more powerful around the shoulders. He was also aggressive, as Steve discovered when the ref dropped the puck and blew the face-off whistle.

Curt moved like a dart, taking the puck and passing it quickly to a wingman. The fine play drew a loud cheer for the black-uniformed Condors' center, and a few scattered boos for Steve.

"A little slow, weren't you?" a fan needled him.

Forgetting how he had felt before the game, Steve was suddenly determined that he wasn't going to let Curt get away with it. He hightailed it toward the Chariots' net with flecks of ice spurting up from his skates like tiny chips, zipped past Hal and Nick, and got to the puck carrier. Reaching out his stick, Steve rammed into the Condor with a hip-jarring check that knocked the player off balance. He grabbed the puck, circled and started to head back toward center ice when Curt almost met Steve head-on. With a snap of his stick, Steve passed the disk to Mark.

Almost at the same instant Curt hit him, then stayed glued to him as they glided across the ice till they crashed against the boards.

"So you're one of those great Chariot players, are

you?" Curt said to him just before they broke apart. "Well, we'll see."

Both of them sprinted up the ice, crossing the neutral zone into Condors' territory where Mark had just passed the puck to Nick. Nick stickhandled the puck along the side of the ice, then passed it to Hal. Just as Hal received it, a Condor defenseman checked him, making him lose control of the puck. The other defenseman skated up, grabbed the puck, and started to carry it back toward center ice.

Noticing Curt in between him and the defenseman, Steve could see the next move coming. Putting on a burst of speed he got in front of Curt at almost the same instant that the defenseman passed the puck. Steve reached out his stick, hooked the puck and started to swerve out of Curt's path with it when he felt something — the blade of a stick — hook around his ankle. He fell and slid across the ice on his knees, as the whistle shrilled.

He looked around and saw the ref skating toward the timekeeper's bench, holding up a finger and shouting, "Tripping! Number Two!"

A moment later, Curt, his head bowed in disgust, was skating slowly toward the penalty box.

He wasn't in there long, however, for Line One's time on the ice was soon up.

"Nice play, Steve," Mark said as they headed through the gate to sit down and rest. "Especially against that hothead."

"He's good, though," Steve admitted. By now he was sure that neither his Uncle Mike nor his mother and father were at the game. He would have heard them if they were.

At 14:36 Mel Hale socked one into the net for the Chariots' first goal.

"It's our turn," said Mark as Line One returned to the ice for the second time.

In the face-off circle Curt's eyes locked with Steve's. Vengeance lurked in their brown, shining depths. Then both centers turned their attention to the spot between them, tension building up as they waited for the ref's whistle.

Shreeek! The puck dropped. This time the sticks struck at the disk simultaneously, and Steve could feel his opponent's strength in his stick. *I wonder how many sticks he's broken so far this year?* Steve thought, not too amused.

But Curt's stick didn't break as he won the scramble and passed the puck to a wingman. Again cheers rose from the fans for Curt, and boos for Steve. But the Chariots' center took the calls in stride now. He just had to play harder the next time, he reflected.

At 11:02 Curt, taking a long pass from one of his wingmen, took two steps toward the Chariots' net and sent the puck flying past Jason Moore's right knee for a goal. Chariots 1, Condors 1.

A smirk lingered on Curt's face as he looked at Steve in the face-off circle. "One up on you," he said, boasting.

"I know," said Steve.

The puck dropped and the whistle blew. Steve's stick flashed. It struck the puck a fraction of a second before Curt's did and zipped across the ice toward Nick. Steve moved at the same time, sprinting past Curt and over the Condors' blue line in a straight path for the net.

A Condors' defenseman checked Nick, then pokechecked the puck in an effort to grab it. The disk spun away, got up on edge for a second, and rolled. Steve went after it. In a sweeping glide he yanked it toward him with the blade of his stick. In the same continuous motion he shot the puck toward the net.

Like a small, black flying saucer it raised off the ice and flew through the air past the goalie's masked face for a goal. Chariots 2, Condors 1.

Sticks from the Chariots' bench clattered against the boards, drowning out the few cheers that sprang from the fans. Steve, doubtful that they were Chariots' cheers, suspected that they came out of respect for his fine shot.

A grin flickered on his face as he stood in the face-off circle. "We're even," he said to Curt.

"Yeah," Curt mumbled.

A Condors' wingman tied the score with a slap shot seconds before the two minutes were up, and the lines relinquished the ice to Lines Two. Chariots 2, Condors 2.

It wasn't till Line Three got on the ice, though, that the 2 to 2 tie was broken. The Chariots' left defenseman Jerry McMann scored the goal with an assist from left winger Abe Nolan.

The third session went by scoreless. The Chariots led, 3 to 2.

No sooner had the teams skated to their locker rooms for their ten-minute intermission than the thought struck Steve again: I must get to a telephone and call Uncle Mike sometime during, or after, this game. He's got to come and help me get away from Kenneth and his odd-ball cohorts.

But how? he thought. I failed once. How can I expect to get away without getting caught again this time?

**S**teve rested his head back against the door of a locker and closed his eyes. He was tired. But the main reason for his closing his eyes was to think, and to discourage anybody from talking to him.

Could he make the break as the teams started back on the ice? he wondered. Should he wait until the second intermission when the chaperones might not be as cautious? Or should he wait until after the game? He had to do it *sometime*.

I'll wait till the second intermission, he decided. It's possible that we won't be as closely watched then. And I'll just play hockey as if nothing else in the world could be more important.

At face-off, as the second period started, Curt Hilliard looked up and stared at Steve almost in a daze as the Chariots' center grabbed the puck.

Stickhandling it along the red line toward the boards in front of the Condors' bench, Steve controlled the puck as if it were an extension of his stick.

A Condors' wingman was almost upon him before he passed it to Mark. Mark took it across the blue line and passed it to Nick. At the same time Steve bolted down the middle of the ice. Nick spotted him and shot him a pass, then sped on toward the net.

Steve grabbed the puck just as a Condors' defenseman checked him. For a moment lights flashed before his eyes like lightning bugs and he lost sight of the puck. Whirling, he felt and heard the collision of metal as his right skate crashed into another. A player in a black uniform spun and hit the ice.

Then Steve heard the familiar crack of stick meeting puck. He looked around and saw the black disk skimming over the ice into Chariots' territory and past the goal.

Shreeek! went the whistle.

"Icing!" the ref called.

He skated to the puck, scooped it up, and brought it back to the right-hand circle near the Condors' net for a face-off.

Steve and a Condors' defenseman faced off. Once

again Steve grabbed the puck and shot it to Mark. Mark stopped it and smashed it toward the net, but a Condors' man deflected it, getting tangled with Hal Spoon as he did so.

Nick rushed in. His stick flashed.

Crack! The puck blazed past the goalie's left foot into the net. It was 4 to 2, Chariots.

Three seconds after the face-off the lines' two minutes were up.

The next two sessions went by scoreless. Steve, his legs aching in spite of the four-minute rest he had taken while the second and third lines were on the ice, was glad the period had ended.

He hadn't forgotten about his plan, either. Just seconds before the clock had run out he had untied the laces of his skates. It would take only a matter of seconds to slip them off.

Keeping in the middle of the crowd as it funneled out of the gate toward the locker rooms, Steve saw the chaperones, Mr. Healy and Mr. Karpis, standing just outside of the Chariots' locker-room door. It was to the left of the gate; the Condors' was to the right.

Great! thought Steve, as if the world had collapsed on him. The entrance to the rink is to the left!

I can't possibly get out of here without their seeing me!

Then a second breath of hope filled his heart. There, at the bottom of the balcony to his right, was a blazing red sign: EXIT.

Ducking and mixing in with the Condors' players, he headed for the exit. As the players began to swarm into their locker room, Steve removed his skates, straightened up, and bolted down the aisle.

He dropped the skates to the side and rushed around a corner to a door. For a moment his heart seemed to hang in limbo as the fear hit him that the door might be locked.

He tried it. It wasn't. He pulled it open and plunged out into the cold afternoon air.

He raced across the sidewalk and the packed parking lot, then down the street, looking hopefully for a store or telephone booth. There was neither one in sight.

He reached the end of the block, panting from the hard run, and glanced down at his socks; they were coming loose. But he couldn't take the time to remove them now. Every second was a precious gem that could lead him to help and complete safety. It could be his final chance to get away from Kenneth Agard, Jr., for good.

He took a moment to glance behind him, and almost froze.

Coming after him at a fast run was Mr. Healy!

Oh, no! thought Steve, and hurried on. He came to an alley, cut through it, then down a flight of steps that led to a backyard. At the bottom step he stubbed his big toe and fell flat on his stomach. Scrambling to his feet, he started ahead again. But he had gone only about ten feet when strong fingers locked around his arm.

As if this time the world had really collapsed on him, Steve looked around at the dark, icy stare of Mr. Healy.

"I guess I'll have to teach you one way or another that you can't run way," the chaperone said, and raised his right hand.

Steve shut his eyes tight and winced as he waited for Mr. Healy to hit him.

"Hold it right there!" a voice said sharply. "Strike him and I'll make mince meat out of you!"

Steve's eyes shot open. That voice? He hadn't

heard it in a long time, but he'd recognize it any-where!

"Dad!" he cried.

Then he saw his mother, and another man — a tall, dark-haired, gentle-faced man — standing next to his father. "Mom! Uncle Mike!"

Tears glistened in his eyes as he rushed into their arms. When he regained his composure, and knew for sure that this time he was really safe, he said hap-pily, "I didn't think I'd ever see any of you again."

"It was your phone call from Buffalo that started our investigation," Mr. Crandall explained as they headed back for the rink. Ahead of them were Mr. Healy and a tall, slim man whom Steve had been in-troduced to a few minutes ago: Mr. Jason Williams, an FBI man. "The policeman who answered your call did some other calling and finally traced your name back to us. That took a lot of time. It wasn't till a couple of days ago that we found out you played with the Chariots hockey team and that the team was going to play here in Mulberry City."

Steve stared at him. "You didn't know till *just a couple of days ago?*"

"That's right," said his mother, her hazel eyes brimming with warmth now. "We've had the police looking for you since the night you disappeared."

"Well, we had to wait twenty-four hours before the police could put you on the missing persons list," Mr. Crandall explained. "But, that's right. That's how long we've been searching for you."

"I can't believe it!" Steve exclaimed.

"Well, you and all the players for the Chariots were playing under an assumed name," Uncle Mike joined in. "That's what made it so tough for the police and the FBI."

"But Kenneth Agard, Jr., said that we had signed papers," Steve said to his father. "And that you'd be getting a check every month."

"Hogwash," Mr. Crandall snorted. "He had lied all the way through. He's just as corrupt as his father, Kenneth Agard, Sr. They both gambled on a hockey team made up of fine young athletes in hopes of brainwashing them of everything except their desire to play hockey. When the kids reached sixteen they were to be placed with a higher age grouped team for further seasoning before joining Mr. Agard,

Sr.'s, professional team. Mr. Agard, Sr., confessed everything."

"They picked on kids who were excellent skaters, and whose parents could use more money," said Uncle Mike. "But," he added, his eyes twinkling, "they didn't count on a kid loaded with spunk like you."

Steve smiled. "Thanks, Uncle Mike. But what about the other kids? What's going to happen to them?"

"They'll be taken home, of course," answered his mother.

"What about Kenneth, Jr.?" Steve asked. "He's the real brains behind the Chariots hockey team."

"Oh, he'll be taken care of properly, all right," his father said. "He's under age to be punished like an adult, but you can bet your boots he's going to pay for what he's done. The FBI doesn't cater to people who are in the business of kidnapping and forging contracts for illegal purposes."

"Where is he now?" Steve asked. "Has he been arrested yet?"

Mr. Crandall smiled. "Speak of the devil . . . look to your left," he said.

Steve did, and saw Kenneth Agard, Jr., being escorted toward a squad car by two policemen. Suddenly the young coach of the Chariots hockey team paused in his tracks and looked at Steve. For a moment Steve thought that Kenneth was going to say something to him, but he didn't. He turned away, squared his shoulders, and continued to the squad car.

I feel sorry for him, Steve thought. He's got brains. He could have used them to better advantage.

Then he saw Mark Slate coming out of the exit with several of the other players and a tall, square-shouldered man Steve assumed was also an FBI agent. Mark paused for a second, saw Steve, and said something to the man. The man nodded, and Mark turned and came walking toward Steve. He stopped a couple of feet in front of Steve, looking pale and ashamed.

"I'm sorry, Steve," he said. "I guess it took this to make me realize how wrong it all was. I hope you won't hate me."

"I can't hate you, Mark," Steve said. "In spite of

everything, you're still my friend. What are you going to do?"

"Go home," said Mark. "I miss my parents, too, and the rest of my family."

Steve put out his hand. Mark took it. "Good-bye, Steve," he said.

"Good-bye, Mark," said Steve.

Mark turned, and left.

Steve looked at his mother, father, and Uncle Mike, took a deep breath, and sighed.

"Know what I'd like to have right now?" he said, feeling the best that he had felt in a long, long time.

"What?" His mother's eyes were wide, expectant, as if to say anything he asked for he could have.

"A big, fat, juicy hamburger!" he exclaimed.

**THE #1 SPORTS SERIES FOR KIDS**

# Read them all!

Baseball Flyhawk

Baseball Turnaround

The Basket Counts

Body Check

Catch That Pass!

Catcher with a Glass Arm

Catching Waves

Center Court Sting

Centerfield Ballhawk

Challenge at Second Base

The Comeback Challenge

Comeback of the Home Run Kid

Cool as Ice

The Diamond Champs

Dirt Bike Racer

Dirt Bike Runaway

Dive Right In

Double Play at Short

Face-Off

Fairway Phenom

Football Double Threat

Football Fugitive

Football Nightmare

The Fox Steals Home

Goalkeeper in Charge

The Great Quarterback Switch

Halfback Attack*

The Hockey Machine

The Home Run Kid Races On

Hot Shot

Ice Magic

Johnny Long Legs

Karate Kick

The Kid Who Only Hit Homers

*Previously published as Crackerjack Halfback

Lacrosse Face-Off

Lacrosse Firestorm

Line Drive to Short**

Long-Arm Quarterback

Long Shot for Paul

Look Who's Playing First Base

Miracle at the Plate

Mountain Bike Mania

Nothin' But Net

Out at Second

Penalty Shot

Power Pitcher***

The Reluctant Pitcher

Return of the Home Run Kid

Run for It

Shoot for the Hoop

Shortstop from Tokyo

Skateboard Renegade

Skateboard Tough

Slam Dunk

Snowboard Champ

Snowboard Maverick

Snowboard Showdown

Soccer Duel

Soccer Halfback

Soccer Hero

Soccer Scoop

Stealing Home

The Submarine Pitch

The Team That Couldn't Lose

Tennis Ace

Tight End

Top Wing

Touchdown for Tommy

Tough to Tackle

Wingman on Ice

The Year Mom Won the Pennant

All available in paperback from Little, Brown and Company

**Previously published as Pressure Play

***Previously published as Baseball Pals

# TWO PLAYERS, ONE DREAM...
## to win the Little League Baseball® World Series

Read all about Carter's and Liam's journeys in the Little League series
by **MATT CHRISTOPHER.**

**LITTLE, BROWN AND COMPANY**
BOOKS FOR YOUNG READERS

Discover more at lb-kids.com    Available however books are sold.